ASTROSAURS:
THE SUN-SNATCHERS

ASTROSAURS: THE SUN-SNATCHERS

Steve Cole

Illustrated by Woody Fox

First published 2008
by Red Fox, an imprint of
Random House Children's Books
This Large Print edition published by
AudioGO Ltd
by arrangement with
Random House Children's Books 2012

ISBN: 978 1471 306761

British Library Cataloguing in Publication Data available

Printed and bound in Great Britain by
MPG Books Group Limited

*For Matthew and Stevie Howe,
who helped me come up with the
dino-villains in this book.*

*I would also like to thank James Barnes,
who suggested woolly rhinos, and
Laura Waterman for improving the title!*

WARNING!

THINK YOU KNOW ABOUT DINOSAURS?

THINK AGAIN!

The dinosaurs . . .

Big, stupid, lumbering reptiles. Right?

All they did was eat, sleep and roar a bit. Right?

Died out millions of years ago when a big meteor struck the Earth. Right?

Wrong!

The dinosaurs weren't stupid. They may have had small brains, but they used them well. They had big thoughts and big dreams.

By the time the meteor hit, the last dinosaurs had already left Earth for ever. Some breeds had discovered how to travel through space as early as the Triassic period, and were already enjoying a new life among the stars. No one has found evidence of dinosaur technology yet. But the first fossil bones were only unearthed in 1822, and new finds are being made all the time.

The proof is out there, buried in the ground.

And the dinosaurs live on, way out in space, even now. They've settled down in a place they call the Jurassic Quadrant and over the last sixty-five million years they've gone on evolving.

The dinosaurs we'll be meeting are part of a special group called the Dinosaur Space Service. Their job is to explore space, to go on exciting missions and to fight evil and protect the innocent!

These heroic herbivores are not just dinosaurs.

They are *astrosaurs*!

NOTE: The following story has been translated from secret Dinosaur Space Service records. Earthling dinosaur names are used throughout, although some changes have been made for easy reading.

THE CREW OF THE DSS SAUROPOD

**CAPTAIN
TEGGS STEGOSAUR**

ARX ORANO,
FIRST OFFICER

GIPSY SAURINE,
COMMUNICATIONS
OFFICER

IGGY TOOTH,
CHIEF
ENGINEER

JURASSIC QUADRANT

Ankylos

Steggos

Diplox

INDEPEN
DINOSA
ALLIAN

VEGETARIAN
SECTOR

Squawk
Major

PTEROSAU

DSS
UNION OF
PLANETS

Tri System

Corytho   Lambeos

Iguanos

Aqua Minor

SEA

OUTER SPACE

Geldos Cluster

Teerex Major

Olympus

TYRANNOSAUR
TERRITORIES

CARNIVORE
SECTOR·

Raptos

lanet Sixty

THEROPOD EMPIRE

Megalos

VEGMEAT
ZONE
(NEUTRAL SPACE)

E SPACE

**Pliosaur
Nurseries**

Not to scale

CHAPTER ONE

THE DISAPPEARING SUN

The spaceship soared through the purple skies like a silver egg hurled by a giant. Over yellow fields and deep green mountains it raced, glinting in the light of two huge suns.

It was the DSS *S a u r o p o d*, finest in the fleet of the Dinosaur Space Service. And it was going faster than it had ever gone before . . .

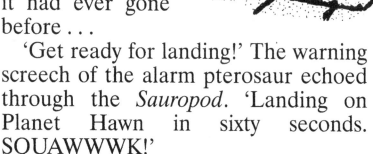

'Get ready for landing!' The warning screech of the alarm pterosaur echoed through the *Sauropod*. 'Landing on Planet Hawn in sixty seconds. SQUAWWWK!'

'About time too!' cried Captain Teggs Stegosaur, ready to charge from

1

his ship the moment they landed. He peered out through a porthole. Far below, the native woolly rhinos were tending their buttercup fields, and Teggs's tummy rumbled loud enough to shake the corridor. Buttercups were the tastiest treats in the entire Jurassic Quadrant, and Teggs was always as hungry for food as he was for adventure!

'Doesn't *look* like there's a terrible emergency here,' Teggs said in surprise. 'I wonder why Admiral Rosso called us so urgently.'

Rosso was the crusty old barosaurus

in charge of the DSS. Only hours earlier, he had summoned the *Sauropod* to Hawn on a double-triple-mega-red-crimson-super-scarlet alert. And Teggs knew that alerts didn't come much redder than that . . . As the ship's landing jets kicked in, he felt a tingle travel through his long spiky tail at the thought of the adventure that must surely lie ahead.

'Captain Teggs!' Gipsy, his stripy hadrosaur communications officer, was hurrying towards him. 'I've just had a message from Admiral Rosso. He will meet us here at the launch pad in exactly two minutes.'

A green, sharp-eyed triceratops appeared just behind her—this was Arx, Teggs's first officer. 'Admiral Rosso wants to tell us about the emergency at once, Captain,' he explained. 'He doesn't want to waste a single second.'

'Neither do I!' Teggs declared. 'Let's eat our dinner during the meeting to save time.'

'Dinner?' Gipsy frowned. 'But, Captain, it's not even lunchtime yet.'

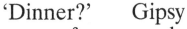

'You're right,' said Teggs, smiling dreamily at the thought of fresh buttercups. 'We should eat lunch, dinner and a

4

midnight supper during the meeting to save even *more* time!'

The *Sauropod* trembled as it touched down on the launch pad. Teggs whacked his tail against a control in the wall and the main doors slid open. He jumped outside through the swirling exhaust smoke and started charging down the ramp.

'Hey, wait for me!' came a gruff voice from inside the *Sauropod*. Seconds later, a brown-and-white iguanodon burst through the smoke—it was Iggy Tooth, the *Sauropod*'s chief engineer. 'I've been pushing the engines as fast as they'll go,' he said, wiping sweat from his brow. 'We've crossed four solar systems in two hours—and I'm dying to know why!'

'We all are,' Arx agreed, as he and

Gipsy came down the ramp to join Teggs and Iggy.

'Well, stand by for answers,' said Teggs, pointing. 'Here comes Admiral Rosso now!'

The smoke was fading to reveal the extraordinary sight of a 23-ton barosaurus flying towards them on a space-scooter. A woolly rhino in a billowing blue cape rode beside him, with a smaller rhino trailing just behind.

'Ahoy there, astrosaurs!' Rosso called.

Teggs and his crew saluted and ran down the ramp as the admiral came into land with his companions.

Rosso's little head bobbed about on the end of his neck, which was as long as a firefighter's hose and three times as thick. 'Captain Teggs, Arx, Gipsy and Iggy . . . Allow me to introduce the ruler of Hawn—Prime Rhino Serras.'

'Thank you for coming,' said Serras politely, shivering a little in her cape. She was a regal-looking woolly rhino with a chocolate-brown coat and big, sad eyes. She turned to the skinny grey

rhino in the roll-neck sweater standing behind her. 'This is my personal assistant, Noss.'

Noss blinked at them through a pair of thick glasses. 'I've been working for Serras for five months, two days and three-and-a-half hours precisely!' he told them proudly.

'I'm pleased to meet you both,' said Teggs. He bowed, grabbing a couple of mouthfuls of the lush yellow grass growing round the launch pad as he did so. 'But, Admiral, what's the terrible emergency?'

'Yes, everything seems wonderful

here,' Arx agreed. 'The air is so cool and fresh . . .'

Gipsy nodded. 'And the buttercup fields look so lovely, lit by the two suns . . .'

'That's just the problem!' snapped Serras.

'Eh?' Iggy frowned. 'Lovely buttercups, a problem?'

Rosso shook his head. 'Two suns, you say, Gipsy? Last week, there were *three* of them!'

For a few moments, the astrosaurs stood in staggered silence.

Teggs found his voice first. 'You mean . . . three suns set one night and only two rose up the next morning?'

'That's exactly what he means,' said Noss sadly, tapping at a large calculator. 'It happened three-point-four-seven-nine days ago and—'

9

'Our sun has gone,' said Serras, interrupting him. 'There is not a trace remaining.'

'But that's impossible,' Arx spluttered. 'How can a sun simply disappear? It's a star—a super-massive ball of fiery gasses, millions of miles across!'

'Nevertheless,' said Rosso, 'Hawn's smallest sun *has* vanished—snatched in the night, while the woolly rhinos slept. When they woke up, they panicked.'

Serras nodded. 'You see, before this, our world was a tropical paradise. We were happy and hot here. Now we must wrap up to keep out the cold.'

'And don't forget, Your Primeness,' said Noss quickly, 'our buttercups need plenty of light and warmth. If any more of our sunlight disappears, our farms will fail.'

'I had not forgotten, Noss.' Serras blinked away a tear. 'My people might starve to death—if they don't freeze to death first!'

'Naturally, Serras called for me at once,' said Rosso. 'I came here in my private starship and was very glad to

learn my finest astrosaurs were only a few solar systems away.'

'Don't worry,' said Teggs. 'We'll get to the bottom of this mystery. Whole suns *can't* just vanish without a trace!'

But even as he spoke, the sky got suddenly darker. In the same split-second, the air became as cold as a ghostly breath. Noss and Serras clomped about in a woolly panic. Even Rosso squealed in disbelief.

'Captain, LOOK!' gasped Iggy.

Teggs knew it wasn't safe to stare into a dazzling bright sun. But the biggest of Hawn's suns was not dazzling bright any longer. It hung in the sky like a chewed orange—almost half of it had been ripped clean away!

11

'Oh, no!' howled Noss. 'At least forty-three-point-five per cent of Hawn Sun Two has been removed!'

'Come on, crew,' Teggs commanded. 'Into the *Sauropod*. Whatever's snatching the suns, it must still be up there in local space.'

Iggy nodded grimly. 'And if it's strong enough to shred a star, think what it could do to *us*!'

'I'm trying not to,' Teggs admitted, his heart pounding with excitement as he led the charge back up the ramp and into the ship. 'Stand by for blast off—we've got a planet to save!'

CHAPTER TWO

ATTACK OF THE SPACE MONSTER

With his crew right behind him, Captain Teggs burst into the *Sauropod*'s flight deck so quickly he smashed through the doors!

'Instant take off!' he yelled.

Teggs's flight crew of flying reptiles—fifty dynamic dimorphodon—flapped into action. They tweaked levers with their claws, and bashed buttons with their beaks. Smoke and flames poured from the *Sauropod*'s jet rockets and the mighty ship shot upwards into space.

'Set a course for Hawn Sun Two,' snapped Teggs, leaping into his control pit. 'Iggy—give us maximum speed!'

Iggy nodded, his claws clicking quickly over the controls. The ship was soon pulsing with extra power as it sped on its way.

Gipsy scrambled into her seat. 'But, Captain, suns are super-hot—won't we melt?'

'We have extra-strong safety-tinted solar shields,' Arx reminded her.

Even so, as the *Sauropod* z o o m e d onwards through space it began to grow very warm.

Sweat was soon dripping down the astrosaurs' scaly backs.

Despite the heat, Arx kept cool. 'We are now one million miles from Hawn Sun Two,' he reported.

'Slow down the engines,' said Teggs. 'And switch on the scanner!'

Sprite, the leader of the dimorphodon, cheeped and flicked a switch. The scanner screen showed them the view outside through the solar shields—a bright, broiling half-chewed ball of blinding fire.

Then, as they watched, a squiggling blaze of light curled away from the savaged sun. It started twisting and

14

twirling towards them.

'What's that?' said Iggy, frowning. 'It looks like a gigantic twitching tadpole!'

Gipsy screwed up her nose as the sinister shape came wriggling closer. 'Or some sort of revolting wormy thing . . .'

'But nothing can survive that close to a sun without being frazzled to a frizzle,' said Arx. 'Er . . . can it?'

'Apparently it can!' Teggs's eyes were shining with wonder. 'I think I know what that thing might be . . .'

The others all looked at him—but then Gipsy jumped about a mile in the air and her headphones flew across the room. 'Oww!' she yelled. 'I heard a terrible screech—it must have come from somewhere close by.'

15

Iggy pointed at the scanner screen. '*I think it came from that!*'

The wriggling shape had sped suddenly closer. It was not a titanic tadpole or a weird worm. It was an enormous menacing monster. Its segmented body coiled and uncoiled, shining like fiery gold. Stubby spikes stuck out all over it like fins. Its face was long and pointy, with red burning eyes and jaws that stretched on for hundreds of miles.

Jaws that were opening wide . . .

16

'Look at that gruesome gob,' cried Iggy. 'You could fit a moon in there!'

'Wait,' said Gipsy, pointing at the screen. 'What's that?'

A ball of dazzling white light was forming in the monster's mouth, growing larger and larger.

Arx checked his controls. 'Sensors say it's a planet-sized ball of intense solar energy—with a temperature of one million degrees centigrade!'

Suddenly the monster jerked its head—and sent the ball of scorching energy searing through space towards the *Sauropod*!

'That star-fire is too hot to handle,' Teggs bellowed. 'Get us out of here— NOW!'

The dimorphodon fell screeching on the controls and the *Sauropod* throbbed with power. But already, the ball of star-fire was about to engulf them.

'No good!' gasped Arx. 'We can't escape in time.'

Gipsy stared in horror at the screen. 'We're going to get roasted!'

CHAPTER THREE

DESPERATE MISSION

'Hang on!' yelled Iggy, flipping back a special cover to reveal a red lever. 'I'll hit the emergency power boost.'

'Quick, Iggy!' Teggs cried. The sizzling fireball was about to hit.

Iggy tugged on the lever—and with a spluttering roar, the *Sauropod* whizzed away, wildly out of control! Teggs was hurled against Arx, who was sent staggering into Gipsy. Iggy almost squashed a dozen dimorphodon as he fell forward onto his nose. A wave of dreadful heat swept through the flight deck.

Then the growl of the engines died down, and the *Sauropod* stopped.

Teggs cheered. 'You did it, Iggy!'

'But half the ship's engines have overloaded!' Iggy sighed. 'We'll have to chug back to Hawn on minimum power and make repairs.'

Arx checked his space radar. 'Luckily that fireball is flying harmlessly out into deep space,' he reported. 'But our giant friend seems to have vanished completely.'

'I think it was a solawurm,' said Teggs slowly.

'A who-what?' said Gipsy.

'I'll explain later,' said Teggs, chomping on some ferns from his control pit. 'Right now we must get back to Admiral Rosso, tell him what's happened and work out a plan . . . before it's too late!'

*   *   *

An hour later, the *Sauropod* was back on Hawn. It was only lunchtime, but with so much of the sun ripped away it seemed more like late evening. Rosso took the astrosaurs to Shaggy Palace, the Prime Rhino's grand headquarters, for a top-secret super-important meeting and some food.

Serras sat at the end of a large yellow table with a woolly bobble-hat on her head. Noss sat beside her in an extra sweater, hugging his calculator for warmth. Both of them were shivering.

22

And as Teggs described the *Sauropod*'s close call in space, they started to shiver even harder.

'A solawurm you say?' asked Serras. 'What are they? Where do they come from?'

'No one knows for sure,' said Teggs through a mouthful of <u>moss.</u> 'But they were first discovered by the Jurassic Explorers, hundreds of years ago. Show them, Arx.'

He waited as Arx loaded up the Jurassic Explorers' Space Index on a computer. The Explorers were Teggs's heroes. They had <u>mapped</u> out most of the Jurassic Quadrant, discovering all kinds of curious creatures as they did so. As a dino-tot, Teggs had been thrilled to hear the tales of their adventures—and one of his favourites concerned a certain giant, wriggly, fire-breathing space-monster . . .

The computer soon showed a picture of a solawurm, taken by one of the Jurassic Explorers.

It looked exactly like the monster that had menaced the *Sauropod*. Noss was so shocked at the sight that he threw his calculator in the air.

'According to the Explorers, solawurms are ultra-rare, mysterious monsters that feed on solar energy,' Teggs explained. 'Although large, fearsome and highly dangerous, they are actually quite peaceful

24

creatures who eat only dying suns with no planets.'

'Peaceful?' said Serras crossly. 'So how come this one is eating *our* suns?'

'Maybe it is confused,' Teggs suggested.

'How did the Explorers find out so much about the horrible things without being fried?' asked Gipsy.

'Luckily, they discovered that solawurms are easily hypnotized,' Teggs revealed.

Serras frowned. 'Hypnotized? What do you mean?'

'Oooh, I've read about this!' said Noss. 'When you hypnotize someone, you soothe them into a sleep-like state. Then you can make them do whatever you want them to.'

He picked up his calculator and peered at it through his thick glasses. 'Mind you, there is a twelve-point-three-four per cent chance that the hypnotized person will start coming to his senses, and—'

'Anyway,' said Teggs quickly. 'The Explorers were trying to get past two solawurms in a shuttle, zipping from left to right, looking for a gap. Before they knew it, the solawurms were hypnotized! They stayed nice and quiet and did whatever the Explorers asked for several days . . .'

'All very interesting, Teggs,' said Rosso gruffly. 'But Serras is right. The solawurm is a deadly threat. I've scanned this part of space and found a trail of half-eaten s u n s stretching for billions of miles.'

S e r r a s

26

stamped two of her large, woolly feet. 'If that monster eats any more of *our* suns we are finished!'

'We are putting our finest crops into special greenhouses for now,' said Noss, tapping at his calculator. 'But if the sunlight gets even eleven per cent dimmer, nothing can save them. We will all be doomed.'

'And where else might this solawurm strike?' Serras added. 'All the Vegetarian Sector is in danger!'

Rosso sighed gloomily. 'I can't take any chances. And so, I have summoned the entire DSS fleet here to Hawn.'

Teggs frowned. 'All five hundred ships?'

'Every last one,' Rosso agreed. 'Their mission will be to drive away that solawurm—or to destroy it!'

'But, Admiral,' Teggs protested, 'solawurms are so rare. They are endangered animals—'

'They are endangering *us!*' said Serras shrilly.

'They are incredibly powerful,' Arx added. 'If attacked, there could be terrible bloodshed.'

'Admiral, let me go after the solawurm and try to hypnotize it as the Explorers did,' Teggs pleaded. 'Maybe I can get it to leave in peace.'

Rosso looked unsure. 'You will be taking a big risk, Teggs.'

'I will be taking a big supply of snacks too,' said Teggs with a crooked smile. 'Come on, Admiral! Risks are all part of an astrosaur's job.'

'Very well,' said Rosso. 'The fleet will not arrive for another forty-eight hours. You can have until then to find this solawurm and tackle it in your own way.'

'But the *Sauropod* isn't repaired yet,'

Iggy reminded them.

'I'll take a shuttle, just like the Jurassic Explorers did,' Teggs declared. 'A small ship will be harder to hit if things get a little . . . *heated*.'

'I'm coming with you, Captain,' said Gipsy firmly. 'Perhaps I can help you communicate with that solawurm.'

Teggs nodded. 'I'll be very glad of the company too!' Then he jumped up from his c h a i r , sending it flying. 'Arx, Iggy, stay here and hurry along those repairs to the *Sauropod*. Gipsy, you come with me.' He saluted Rosso and the woolly rhinos, then dashed from the room. 'We will see you soon!'

'I hope so,' Arx murmured sadly. He knew that Teggs and Gipsy had just left on the most dangerous mission of their

lives—and that they might never return
. . .

CHAPTER FOUR

THE SOLAWURM STRIKES

Teggs and Gipsy fired up Shuttle Alpha, the *Sauropod*'s fastest mini-ship. 'Dung-burners set to maximum,' Gipsy reported. 'We have stink-off!'

Teggs whooped as the smelly engines sent them hurtling through the planet's atmosphere and out into space, in search of the solawurm.

'How are we going to find it?' Gipsy wondered.

'Something that big will be hard to miss!' said Teggs. 'Let's see if we can pick up its trail.'

It wasn't long before they saw signs of the solawurm's savage star-scoffing spree. Frozen planets spun about half-chewed suns. Scorched moons and asteroids hung in space like burned coals. One star had been split open like a grapefruit, its fire spilling out through space for thousands of miles.

Teggs gazed out on the destruction

and nervously switched on the shuttle's solar-shield for added protection.

'That solawurm is the scariest thing I have ever seen,' Gipsy declared. 'I shall never forget the way it screeched when it saw the *Sauropod*.'

'It's *incredibly* scary,' Teggs agreed. 'But if the DSS fleet attack it, there will be a big battle and many astrosaurs could be killed. We have to try to stop the solawurm peacefully if we can.'

They flew on and on, into the fringes of the

Vegmeat Zone—the no-man's land between plant-eater space and the Carnivore Sector.

'Captain, *look*!' cried Gipsy. 'Over there!'

Teggs squinted at the distant stars—and then gulped as a familiar, wriggling shape uncurled from behind a planet. It started sniffing at the remains of a once-bright sun, now reduced to cinders.

'We've found the solawurm,' Teggs breathed. 'Let's just hope it's happy to be hypnotized!'

Slowly, carefully, he steered the shuttle closer to the super-sized sun-swallower . . .

*　　　*　　　*

Back on Hawn, Arx was sitting in the Shaggy Palace with Noss, watching the news on TV.

None of it was good.

Serras was giving brave speeches all over the planet, urging the woolly rhinos to stay calm and promising warm jumpers for everyone. But the population was in a panic. Their lush fields of buttercups were dying in the cold, or being washed away by heavy rains. Seaside towns stood deserted because no one wanted to go on holiday—there was nowhere warm and bright on the whole planet. The rhinos' woolly coats were wet not only with the rain, but with tears.

Noss sighed. 'According to my calculations, your Captain has only a ten per cent chance of even *finding* the solawurm, let alone hypnotizing it.'

'There's more to life than just calculations!' said Arx stiffly.

S u d d e n l y, Iggy burst into the room, his scaly hide filthy with oil. 'The repairs are coming along too slowly,' he growled. 'Arx, that rewiring you did has fixed  the computers a treat. But two of the engines still need to be rebuilt from scratch.' He clomped over to the window, scowling at the miserable day outside. 'This was such a sunny, happy place. Now look at it—dismal as a dung heap!'

'At least thirty-two per cent *more* dismal,' Noss agreed sadly.

Just then, Arx's communicator bleeped. 'It's a space message from Shuttle Alpha!' the triceratops announced.

Iggy bounced over. 'What does it say?'

'It's an update from Gipsy. They've found the solawurm sniffing about the

Vegmeat Zone and they're going to try and hypnotize it.' Arx smiled at Noss. 'See? Beating the odds is what astrosaurs do best!'

'I hope so,' said Noss, turning anxiously back to his calculator. 'Because the chances of Teggs and Gipsy surviving a solawurm encounter are just *two* per cent!'

'Of course they will survive!' snapped Iggy. 'And they will soon stop that solawurm eating any more of your suns. Won't they, Arx?'

'Wait a minute . . .' Now Arx was staring out the window too. 'If the solawurm is being hypnotized in

36

the Vegmeat Zone . . . *what is that thing up there?*'

Arx and Noss ran over to the window in alarm. Snaking through the sky, the sinister shadow of a solawurm was circling the remains of Hawn's suns!

'Bless my head-frill!' Arx gulped. 'There must be TWO solawurms—one in the Vegmeat Zone with Teggs and Gipsy, and one right here!'

Noss's calculator blew up. 'We've had it!' the woolly rhino wailed, and fainted.

Iggy stared helplessly at the twisting terror in the gloomy sky. 'Somehow we've got to scare off that solar scavenger, before all Hawn freezes over!'

'With the *Sauropod* out of action, there's nothing we can do,' Arx whispered. 'It looks like the whole planet is doomed—and us along with it!'

CHAPTER FIVE

SHOWDOWN IN SPACE

Out in the Vegmeat Zone, in their tiny shuttle, Teggs and Gipsy were drawing ever nearer to their deadly destination. They were so nervous they barely dared to breathe. The blazing solawurm was still hanging there in space with its spiky back to them, sniffing at some solar cinders.

'It's going to see us at any moment, Gipsy,' said Teggs. 'And when it does, I'm going to have to swing the ship from side to side in front of its eyes—like hypnotists swing a pendant to put people under their spell . . .'

But suddenly, as if it could hear Teggs's whispered words, the solawurm turned round to face them!

'Captain!' Gipsy gasped. 'Look at that face, those eyes . . . Don't you see it?'

Teggs frowned. The solawurm looked just as terrifying as before,

except . . . there was something slightly different about it. Its eyes were not red, but a deep indigo, glittering like the stars it fed upon. It had longer spikes on its head, and its golden, smoking jaws were marked with deep red stripes.

'Good grief!' Teggs breathed. 'This isn't the same solawurm we tackled at Hawn. It's a different one altogether!'

'I thought you said they were rare?' said Gipsy.

'They *are* rare,' Teggs insisted. 'But we will wind up *well done* if we don't start hypnotizing it fast!' He turned to the thrust controls. 'Stand by to activate the shuttle's side jets—fire them for two seconds one way, then two the other.'

'Firing now,' said Gipsy, and the shuttle lurched to the left.

'And again, the other way!' cried Teggs.

Gipsy hit another switch with her hoof and they swung back again in a semicircle, this time to the right.

'Left again!' Teggs ordered. 'Good—now, right again!'

The solawurm watched them swinging from side to side.

'I'm getting space-sick,' groaned Gipsy, her head-crest flushing green.

'Keep going,' Teggs urged her. 'I think it's working!'

The solawurm's eyes were rolling from side to side as it kept the shuttle in sight. But its gaze was getting glassy. Its enormous eyelids were starting to droop.

'Now what?' hissed Gipsy.

'Let's go into reverse and hope the solawurm will follow us,' Teggs suggested. He hooked his spiky tail over the reverse jet controls, and the shuttle s t a r t e d m o v i n g backwards as it swung from side to side. 'Keep steady on the side jets!'

'It's working,' Gipsy squealed, as the sleepy solawurm started wriggling after them. 'But where can we lead it to—and can we ever get away without it waking up again?'

'One ridiculously large problem at a time, Gipsy,' Teggs told her firmly.

But they were so intent on leading the mesmerized menace away, they didn't notice a small, scorched asteroid float into view behind them—until it was too late.

CRUMMMP! The back of the shuttle bashed against the sooty space-rock, and Teggs and Gipsy were flung

41

forward onto the controls. Teggs's beak hit a switch and the ship lurched to the side, spinning around in a wild circle.

'Oh, no!' he cried, frantically twisting dials and pulling levers as they spun about. 'We must get the shuttle back under control!'

Gipsy batted some buttons with her hooves. 'I've shut down the dung-burners,' she reported. 'But *look*! The solawurm's woken up!'

Teggs saw that she was right—the shuttle's jerky movements had snapped the monster out of its light trance. Its

g l i t t e r i n g
eyes were
open wide,
and its face
was twisted
with anger.
It opened its
jaws, and
a ball of
b l a z i n g
white light
began to
form there,
g r o w i n g
larger and

fiercer with every passing moment . . .

'Time we were going!' cried Teggs. He tried to restart the engines—but they only spluttered and coughed. 'Oh, no! The dung-burners won't switch on again. That asteroid we bumped into must have damaged them!'

By now, the dazzling white flame-ball in the monster's throat was the size of a small moon.

'I'll try to communicate,' said Gipsy desperately, switching on the shuttle's space-speakers. 'Solawurm, try to understand me,' she called in a shaky voice. 'We mean you no harm. Please don't fry us to a frazzle!'

But the giant monster only snarled and opened its giant jaws wider. Flames and smoke were gushing from its mouth.

'I can't get through to it!' Gipsy's head-crest flushed neon blue as she clutched hold of Teggs. 'Goodbye, Captain—it looks like this is the end!'

CHAPTER SIX

A MEETING OF MINDS

In the gardens of the Shaggy Palace, Admiral Rosso watched helplessly as the solawurm nibbled the surviving scraps of Hawn Sun Two. From this distance, millions of miles away, the solawurm looked more like a tiny tadpole in the sky than the most dangerous animal in the universe.

Fresh back from her whirlwind tour of the planet, Prime Rhino Serras sat shivering beside him. 'You star-swallowing menace!' she bellowed up at the sky.

'Just you wait till my fleet arrives!' Rosso added. But until then, he knew he was utterly helpless. There was very little of the second sun left. Only Hawn Sun Three still shone fully in the grey sky, and alone it wasn't enough to warm and light such a large planet.

Suddenly he saw Arx and Iggy running towards him.

'Admiral!' Iggy panted. 'We've heard from Teggs. He's tackling another solawurm out in the Veg-meat Zone!'

Serras's bobble-hat shot up in the air. 'You mean there are *two* of them?'

'At least two,' Arx confirmed. 'I'm sure that's the first one we saw up there. We thought it had flown far away—but it must have hidden behind the third sun, waiting to strike again.'

'If only the *Sauropod* was repaired,' cried Iggy.

'A single ship can do little against something so powerful,' said Rosso. 'We must wait for the fleet to arrive, and hope that five hundred ships can handle two solawurms at once . . .'

'Hey, look!' called Arx, pointing to the sinister shape in the sky. 'He's off!'

Leaving nothing but a few blazing specks to mark where the second sun had been, the solawurm wriggled away,

47

twisting back out into space.

'I wonder where it will go now,' said Serras gravely.

Arx's communicator beeped. He held it to his ear as a cheepy-chirpy noise came out. 'It's Sprite, on the *Sauropod*,' the triceratops explained. 'He says the solawurm is heading straight for the Vegmeat Zone at five thousand miles an hour . . .'

'Then . . . it must be going after Teggs and Gipsy!' Iggy buried his face in his claws. 'One tiny shuttle against two of those monsters at once? They won't stand a chance!'

*   *   *

Unaware of this fresh menace now streaking towards them from Hawn, Teggs and Gipsy were clinging onto each other, waiting for the star-fire to burst from the solawurm's smoking

48

jaws.

'Wait! There's just one tiny chance!' cried Teggs. 'Gipsy, that screech that the first solawurm made . . . can you do an impression of it?'

'Why?' asked Gipsy.

Teggs shrugged. 'If this one thinks we speak its language, it might not burn us to a crisp!'

'OK, I'll try,' Gipsy agreed. 'Now, how did it go . . .?' She cleared her throat, ran to the communicator, threw back her head . . .

And performed the most incredible, howling, hooting shriek that Teggs had ever heard! It was so loud and screechy that his ears nearly popped. On and on it went, until at last Gipsy ran out of puff and sank gasping to the floor.

Teggs helped her back into her seat. 'That was an amazing impression,' he told her. 'And it's *made* an impression on the solawurm—look!'

Through the shuttle's windscreen, Gipsy saw the last of the star-fire was being sucked back down inside the solawurm's throat. It stared at the little ship with a curious look in its deep blue eyes.

Then, quite suddenly, the astrosaurs heard a low, booming voice. They seemed to hear not with their ears . . .

but with their *minds*.

'Help?' The big voice inside their heads sounded puzzled. 'Did you just call for help in my own language?'

'Who said that?' Teggs demanded, looking all around.

'I did, you silly dinolings!' said the deep voice in their heads. Through the shuttle windscreen, they saw the solawurm *wave* to them! 'I am communicating with you through the power of thought. My name is Heelum.'

'Captain,' Gipsy gasped. 'Do you know what this means?'

Teggs nodded. 'It means the solawurm can talk with us using its mind.'

'Of course I can!' said Heelum, looking very lofty. 'I can hear your thoughts and send you my own as easy as solar pie!'

'Then why didn't you speak sooner?'

asked Teggs. 'Why try to fry us?'

'Because you were trying to hypnotize and trick me, and I lost my temper,' said Heelum sharply. 'I don't listen to *anything* when I'm angry.'

'Captain, do you know what *else* this means?' said Gipsy excitedly. 'It means that the first solawurm we met wasn't shouting in anger . . . it was shouting for *help*!'

'And that is the only reason I am not roasting you right now, puny dinolings,' boomed the echoing voice in their heads. 'Because if you know *any* of my language you must have met my little brother!'

Teggs frowned. 'Your brother?'

'His name is Grakk, and we are the only solawurms in this part of space,' said Heelum. 'He's got red eyes and is slightly less spiky than me.'

'We've met him all right,' said Teggs grimly. 'If he's not stopped he's going

52

to wipe out all life on Planet Hawn by eating its suns, one after another!'

'YOU LIE!' Heelum spoke so loudly that Gipsy and Teggs thought their heads might burst. 'We solawurms never eat the suns of living worlds. We are peaceful creatures—unless we are provoked.'

'Well, perhaps Grakk has forgotten that,' said Gipsy. 'We thought *you* were a danger too. That's why we tried to hypnotize you.'

'I remember,' said Heelum, with a distant look in his eyes. 'The Jurassic Explorers hypnotized us, many centuries ago. Using the power of thought, they sent us far, far away from this part of the galaxy . . .'

Teggs frowned. 'So what are you

doing back again?'

'I told you, puny dinoling—looking for my brother. He went missing weeks ago and—' Suddenly, Heelum broke off. 'Wait. Here he comes now!'

Teggs and Gipsy ran to the shuttle window and looked out. Sure enough, a solawurm was approaching. But he did not look very well. His skin was no longer golden, but pale and smothered in thick smoke. His red eyes were bulging and full of steam. And he was so enormously fat, he looked as if he'd been stuffed.

'Grakk!' cried Heelum, swimming through space to greet his podgy brother. 'Where have you been? I've been so worried about you . . .'

But Grakk did not reply. He just hung there in space, sleepy-eyed, bulging like a vast solawurm sausage.

'He's sick,' Teggs observed. 'It's probably all these suns he's been eating!'

Gipsy was watching Grakk closely. 'He looks like he's in some kind of a trance . . .'

'You are right, dinoling.' Heelum waved his spikes in front of Grakk's bleary eyes but Grakk only burped a small fireball at him. 'He has been hypnotized!'

Teggs was puzzled. 'But if he's hypnotized, how come he shouted for help?'

'Noss said there was a twelve-point-something per cent chance that somebody hypnotized would come to his senses, remember?' said Gipsy. 'Maybe Grakk didn't *want* to eat Hawn's suns . . .'

'But somebody *made* him do it,' Teggs realized.

Gipsy gulped and pointed out the window. 'Somebody like *them*!'

Teggs whirled round to find a fleet of spaceships had crept up on them, unnoticed. But they were like no spaceships he had ever seen. There were ten all together—gigantic, dark and sinister, with giant pendulums swinging slowly from their iron bellies: *Tick . . . tock . . . tick . . . tock . . .* The ships closed in on Heelum in a large semicircle, making him their target.

And then a scary, rasping voice rattled out over the strange ships' space-speakers, chilling Teggs and Gipsy to the bone: 'We turned your brother into our helpless hypnotized slave, solawurm. Now we shall turn *you* into a mindless weapon too!'

CHAPTER SEVEN

HYPNOTIC HORROR

'I don't know where those ships came from or who's on board,' said Teggs, 'but now they're trying to hypnotize Heelum as well as Grakk!'

'We knew Grakk had a brother,' the cold, gloating voice went on. 'We knew he would come searching. And we *definitely* knew we would catch him . . .'

Heelum looked like he was about to lash out at the approaching ships. But suddenly Grakk opened his giant jaws and grabbed hold of his brother. Heelum struggled but he couldn't shake Grakk loose without hurting him. He was stuck fast.

'Don't look at the pendulums, Heelum!' Gipsy yelled as the enormous ships drew closer. '*You mustn't look!*'

But it was too late. *Tick . . . tock . . . tick . . . tock . . .* Heelum's eyes were glazing over. He was being hypnotized! *Tock . . . tick . . .*

'I'm starting to get sleepy myself,' Teggs r e a l i z e d , watching the p e n d u l u m s swing smoothly left to right and back again. *Tick . . . tock . . . tick* . . . He shook his head to try and clear it. 'Gipsy, we *must* get the shuttle started again and . . . Gipsy?'

She didn't answer. Gipsy was already in a trance! And Teggs could feel himself falling under the hypnotic ships' spell as well.

As he f i n a l l y gave into the urge to sleep, he could hear the sound of evil laughter echoing in his ears . . .

*   *   *

When Teggs awoke, he was lying in a bloodstained control room. It was gloomy and hot and the smell of raw meat hung in the air. Teggs tried to jump up—and found he couldn't move. His front legs had been cuffed together and his tail was chained to the wall.

'Ouch—my head!' groaned Gipsy beside him. Teggs saw she had been trussed up in much the same way. 'Where are we?'

'Oh, do be quiet, old girl!' came a cold, posh voice from the shadows. 'On my ship, you speak when you're spoken to. But since you're awake, you twig-nibbling twits, let me shed a little light on your situation . . .'

A blood-red glow filled the room, to reveal a large throne carved from a dinosaur's ribcage. Upon the throne sat a huge, evil-looking carnivore, like a T. rex but with bigger, stronger arms and even nastier teeth. It was wearing a checked velvet dressing gown and a monocle over one eye. Two more of the giant creatures stood on either side of him in smart black suits.

'We've been captured by a bunch of megalosaurus,' hissed Gipsy, with fear in her eyes. 'Some of the deadliest meat-eaters of all time!'

'Not to mention the poshest,' Teggs whispered back.

'You are cut off from all safety on board my private war craft!' gloated the figure on the throne. 'Cower before the might of Lord Rawhead!'

'Lord Rawhead?' Teggs gasped. '*The* Lord Rawhead? The one and only lordliest-lord-of-all-ever-lords Lord Rawhead?'

Rawhead smiled smugly. 'You have heard of me.'

'Of course,' said Teggs. 'Didn't you come top in the Smelliest Carnivore contest six years running? Or was that your mum?'

'S I L E N C E !' roared Rawhead. 'My name is one you leaf-munching losers will come to fear . . . when I have taken over the entire Vegetarian Sector!'

'So *that's* why you're hypnotizing solawurms,' Teggs realized. 'You want them to attack the suns of plant-eater planets!'

'But how did you even find Grakk?' asked Gipsy. 'The Jurassic Explorers sent the solawurms far away.'

'I know,' said Rawhead. 'But knowing what e x c e l l e n t weapons they would make, I decided to bring some of them back! For years, I searched the outermost reaches of the Jurassic Quadrant with long-range space-scopes, building a fleet of hypno-ships ready to capture one. Then, at last, I found Grakk.' Rawhead snapped his jaws. 'It was child's play to hypnotize him into thinking he is evil and bad and starving hungry the whole time.'

'Not the whole time,' Teggs informed him. 'We heard Grakk shout for help.'

Rawhead shrugged. 'The hypnosis may wear off a little after a few days. That is why I called Grakk back here—to put him fully under my control.' The carnivore cackled. 'And now I shall jolly well do the same to his helpless brother.'

'Where *is* Heelum?' Gipsy

demanded.

'See for yourself!' Rawhead clicked his claws and a scanner screen dropped down from the roof. It showed Heelum, hovering sleepily in space, surrounded by the sinister spacecraft. 'He is right outside, held helpless by my hypno-ships. Soon, I need only point him at a sun and he will gobble it up—wiping out the population of every planet that orbits it!'

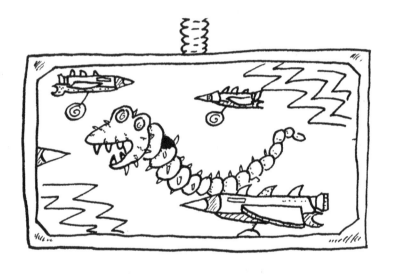

Gipsy closed her eyes and lowered her head.

'You are a cruel tyrant, Rawhead,' said Teggs. 'Solawurms are magnificent wild animals, and you're turning them into bloated killers. Grakk must have dreadful indigestion after eating so many suns.'

'His wind alone could suffocate a small dinosaur colony!' Rawhead agreed. 'But all this sun-snatching is simply a distraction . . .'

Teggs frowned. 'What do you mean?'

'Grakk's attacks are luring the entire DSS fleet to this sector of space. Dealing with a pair of solawurms will keep them tied up for days—leaving DSS Headquarters unguarded.' Rawhead polished his monocle on his grubby sleeve and sniggered. 'Naturally, I shall break in and steal the files on every plant-eating planet. I will discover the secrets of their defences, and all their weak points. *Then*, my carnivore army will invade those planets . . . and conquer the entire Vegetarian Sector!'

'You will never get the knowledge you need from DSS HQ,' said Teggs firmly. 'Our base is *never* left unguarded. Admiral Rosso always sets the burglar alarm when he goes out.'

Rawhead nodded. 'Which is why I shall need a couple of top astrosaurs to help get me inside . . . Shan't I?'

Teggs suddenly realized why the megalosaurus had captured them. 'No!' he cried. 'We will never help you—will we, Gipsy?'

But Gipsy simply covered her eyes with her hooves, and said nothing.

'Sorry, old boy!' Lord Rawhead jumped off his throne and stamped over to Teggs, wiggling his claws and licking his leathery lips. 'If you do not obey me, I will eat your stripy young friend here alive.' He hopped in a circle about Gipsy, drool splashing from his jaws. 'I shall start at her toes, end at her nose, and take her tail for a toothpick! Ha ha ha!'

'You barking mad butcher!' Teggs struggled against his chains with all his

strength, but he could not break free. 'Your plan will fail, just you wait.'

'Afraid not, old chap.' Rawhead smiled. 'Now Grakk has helped me secure his brother, I think it is time he finished the job he started. That way, the DSS fleet will get here all the quicker . . .' He crossed to a large microphone and hit a switch. 'Hypno-ships,' he commanded, 'instruct that overstuffed solawurm to eat Hawn Sun Three—and so destroy the woolly rhino world for ever!'

69

CHAPTER EIGHT

THE FLAMES OF FATE

Wrapped up in a warm coat, Arx sat helplessly in an upstairs room of the Shaggy Palace. Serras, Noss and Admiral Rosso sat just as helplessly beside him.

A long, wide window gave a magnificent view of Hawn's rolling fields—fields that were now white with frost. Dozens of desperate woolly rhinos were digging tunnels in the frozen ground, trying to find shelter

from the dreadful weather. The tiny sun was rising weakly above the horizon.

'How I used to love our three suns in the dawn.' Serras sighed. 'Now, our world is about as bright as our future!'

'The chances of any crops growing on Hawn have fallen to zero,' said Noss, still holding his broken calculator. 'It's too cold and dark.'

'The DSS will help you,' Rosso promised them. 'We shall beat those solawurms, whatever it takes.'

Arx sighed and stared out at the *Sauropod* standing on its launch pad. Iggy was on board right now, working

his claws off to fix the engines. With the DSS fleet not due to arrive for ten hours, and with Teggs and Gipsy still away, the *Sauropod* was Hawn's only defence. And who knew when the next solawurm attack would come?

A beep came from Arx's communicator—and Sprite's worried voice chirped out. His heart sinking, Arx turned to face the others.

'The dimorphodon report that a solawurm has left the Vegmeat Zone,' he reported. 'It is making a beeline straight for Hawn.'

'Then Teggs and Gipsy have failed,' said Rosso sadly.

Serras's horns drooped. 'The solawurm will eat our only sun.'

'We're doomed!' wailed Noss. 'It's one hundred per cent certain!'

But suddenly, a rumbling, thundering noise started up as the *Sauropod*'s powerful jet rockets roared into life.

Arx whooped and spoke into his communicator. 'Iggy—you got the engines working!'

'You bet I have,' came Iggy's joyful voice. 'And they're faster than ever. So jump aboard and let's stop that solawurm!'

'On my way,' Arx told him.

'I'm coming too,' added Rosso.

'And us,' said Serras. She looked at Noss, who nodded nervously.

'CHARRRRGE!' Arx hollered—and with that he jumped out through the window into a tree, slid down the trunk like it was a firefighter's pole and raced away towards the launch pad.

The battle of his life was waiting, and there was no time to lose!

*   *   *

Back on the megalosaurus ship, Teggs and Gipsy were all but forgotten while Lord Rawhead and his favourite officers enjoyed a huge celebration feast.

'Of course, the wonderful thing about snatching suns is that the dinosaurs on the nearest planets are frozen alive,' said Lord Rawhead chattily. 'And so one is left with a world-sized deep-freeze stuffed full of ready meals!'

His minions laughed daintily, before digging into their raw steaks.

'Crummy carnivores,' muttered Teggs. He turned to Gipsy, and saw that she still had her cuffed hooves clutched tightly over her eyes. 'Don't cry, Gipsy,' he murmured kindly.

'I'm not crying, Captain,' Gipsy hissed. 'I've been trying to *concentrate*.'

'On what?' asked Teggs, baffled.

Gipsy nodded towards the scanner screen, which still showed the sleeping solawurm. 'I am trying to get through to Heelum. He communicates using the power of thought, remember? He hears with his mind. Well, I'm thinking *WAKE UP* just as loudly as I can!'

Teggs grinned. 'Gipsy, you're brilliant.'

'Not brilliant enough.' She sighed. 'Those hypno-ships are urging Heelum to stay asleep, and I just can't get through to him.'

'Let's both try,' Teggs whispered. He

76

tried to shout with his mind—'WAKE UP, HEELUM!'

The solawurm did not stir.

'WAKE UP!!!' Teggs imagined the words a hundred miles high in his head.

But Heelum slept on.

'Stuffed diplodocus toes for pudding!' Lord Rawhead announced. 'Help yourselves!'

'Help . . .' Teggs murmured, frowning. 'Gipsy, that's it—your impression of Grakk asking for help!'

'Of course!' hissed Gipsy. 'The thoughts of two little astrosaurs can't mean much to a solawurm. But the sound of his brother in distress . . .'

Trying to shut out the noise of Rawhead's rotten dinner party, Gipsy thought about Grakk's screech for help in all its unbelievable loudness. She replayed it in her mind, again and again, louder and louder . . .

'It's working, Gipsy,' she heard Teggs whisper. 'Heelum's eyelids are twitching. He's starting to wake up! He's . . . UH-OH!'

Suddenly, the whole ship shook and Gipsy's eyes snapped open—in time to see a furious Heelum breathing huge balls of star-fire at the hypno-ships that surrounded him!

Rawhead jumped up in a panic and saw what was happening. 'No!' he shouted, as two of his sinister spacecraft exploded in flames. 'Dash it all, it's impossible!'

'Looks like Heelum has *woken up* to your nasty little plans!' Teggs jeered.

'Shut your trap!' snarled Rawhead, crossing to his special microphone. 'Attention, all remaining hypno-ships! Set pendulum-power to maximum! Put that solawurm back to sleep!'

But the hypno-ship crews were too busy fleeing in panic to listen. Two of the mighty craft got their pendulums tangled together, and started swinging each other around, out of control. They smashed into a third hypno-ship, which exploded . . .

And then, very slowly, Heelum turned to Lord Rawhead's war craft. Eyes blazing with anger, he started to open his incredible jaws.

'Fire up the engines!' Rawhead yelled. 'We must get out of here!'

'You can't outrun a solawurm,' Teggs warned him.

Star-fire formed in the solawurm's cavernous throat.

'No, Heelum!' Gipsy cried. '*We* are on board too!'

'He can't hear you,' said Teggs. 'He never listens when he's angry, remember? There's no stopping him now.'

The astrosaurs watched the scanner in horror as Heelum spat the sizzling star-fire straight at them . . .

CHAPTER NINE

CARNAGE, COLLISIONS AND CHAOS

The dazzling fireball seared through space towards Rawhead's war craft—but just as it was about to hit, an abandoned hypno-ship drifted into its path! CR-RRR-*OOOOSH*! The hypno-ship was blasted to pieces.

'Hurray!' cheered Lord Rawhead, doing a little jig with his officers. 'We're saved!'

'No!' Teggs shouted. 'There's still the wreckage—'

Before he could even finish his sentence, the scorched remains of the hypno-ship smashed into them.

It was like a football, kicked by a woolly mammoth, hitting a meringue.

With an ear-splitting crash the entire war craft was tipped almost upside down. Sirens screamed. The lights flickered.

'Look out, Captain!' Gipsy yelled, as

a dozen megalosaurus were thrown helplessly through the air towards them.

Pulling tight on his chains, Teggs did his best to curl up as small as possible. *OOF! ARGH! SPLAT!* The carnivores' scaly bodies slammed into the walls like massive, meat-eating missiles, badly denting the metal—and weakening it enough for Teggs to finally break free.

'Did it!' he cried, trampling dazed officers underfoot as he rushed to free Gipsy. Stooping to pluck a broken tooth from Lord Rawhead's mouth,

Teggs quickly picked the lock on her cuffs. 'But we're sitting ducks for Heelum's next attack. We have to get out of here.'

Gipsy hugged Teggs tight, then led the way out of the control room. 'Let's find the shuttle bay and hope there's a ship on board we can escape in!'

They staggered off through dark corridors, deafened by the emergency sirens, tossed this way and that as the war craft spun helplessly out of control. At last they reached the shuttle bay.

But the only ship waiting within was their own!

'The dung-burners aren't working!' Gipsy groaned. 'We'll be just as helpless in Shuttle Alpha as we are here!'

'At least we'll be a smaller target,' said Teggs. But the door would not budge. 'Those megalosaurus maniacs have locked it!'

'Indeed we have!' growled a familiar voice behind them. It was Lord Rawhead! 'My hypno-ships may be wrecked, but dear Grakk remains under my control. My plans can still succeed—and I can still stop YOU!'

So saying, he opened his bloody jaws and thundered towards the astrosaurs at top speed. But at the last moment, Teggs dived aside and tripped up Rawhead with his tail. The carnivore toppled and fell headfirst into the shuttle door—smashing it open and knocking himself out!

'Maybe we should call him Lord *Sore*-head from now on!' Teggs joked as he dragged the dinosaur inside.

Gipsy scowled. 'He deserves to be left here.'

'We need him to free Grakk from

that deep hypnotic trance,' Teggs reminded her. He unclipped his belt and used it to tie Rawhead's claws together. 'But first we've got to find a way out . . .'

As Teggs spoke, the heavy doors that stood between the shuttle bay and outer space bent and buckled and burned away—to reveal an enormous dark and glittering eye pressed up close.

Teggs gasped. 'Heelum's here!'

'Where is the swine who hurt my brother and tried to hurt me?' boomed the familiar voice in Teggs and Gipsy's heads.

Gipsy shut her eyes and thought as loudly as she could. 'We have him here and will make him pay for his crimes—but first you must stop Grakk from eating Hawn's last remaining sun.'

'If Grakk eats much more star-fire, he will go pop!' Heelum agreed. 'Very well, dinolings. I will try to stop him. But I don't know where Hawn is.'

'*We* do,' Gipsy yelled in her head. 'It's due north from here. Take us with you and we will guide the way.'

For a long, frightening moment, nothing more was said. Then a thick, black, hairy, vine-like thing curled into the shuttle bay. Teggs gasped. 'What in space is that?'

'One of my eyelashes,' Heelum rumbled, curling it around the shuttle. 'You are so puny and small, any other part of me would squash you flat. Now—*let us fly!*'

The astrosaurs yelled as the shuttle

was yanked away in the grip of Heelum's enormous eyelash. The starry skies blurred about them as they shot off in hot pursuit of the solawurm's brother . . .

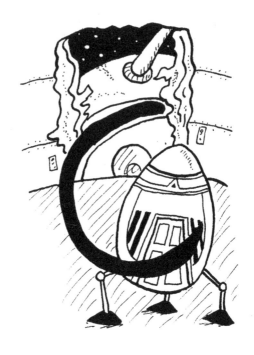

Clinging on grimly to his chair, Teggs knew that hungry, hypnotized Grakk had a huge head start. Could they possibly stop him in time?

CHAPTER TEN

GREAT BALLS OF FIRE!

The heat was stifling on board the *Sauropod* as the spaceship soared ever closer to Hawn Sun Three. Although it was small as stars went, up close it was still far hotter than the most powerful furnace. Nobody spoke—they were all too tense and sweaty. Rosso was squeezed into Teggs's control pit, Noss and Serras were squashed up in Gipsy's place, and Arx, Iggy and the dimorphodon stood at their controls.

'Solawurm dead ahead!' Arx reported, studying his space radar.

'I see it!' Iggy pointed an oily claw at the scanner. The wriggling, squiggling figure was unmistakable. It was heading for the sun.

'We must distract it,' said Rosso.

Arx nodded grimly. 'I shall fire all our dung torpedoes at once.'

'And I'll try the laser cannons at the same time,' said Iggy.

Rosso nodded. 'Fire!'

The torpedoes and lasers zeroed in on Grakk's pale, bloated form. *KER-BOOOOOOOM!* There was a searingly smelly explosion and a cloud of dense brown smoke.

Then the smoke cleared, and Serras and Noss both screamed. The angry solawurm was now coming straight for the *Sauropod*!

'It worked!' cried Arx. 'We distracted him from eating the sun!'

'But now it's two thousand per cent certain he's going to eat *us*!' Noss whimpered.

'Or turn us into blazing wreckage that will rain down all over Hawn,' said Serras, more imaginatively.

Sure enough, a seething ball of star-fire shot from Grakk's throat and came sizzling towards them.

'We're not going up in smoke just yet,' Iggy promised her. 'My souped-up engines will get us clear!' He pulled on a brand-new lever and the *Sauropod* surged with power—power enough to propel them clear of the giant fireball.

Rosso cheered. 'Well done, Iggy!'

'But that thing is still after us!' warned Serras. 'How long can our luck last?'

'Cheer up,' said Iggy brightly. 'At

least our flaming remains will warm up the poor woolly rhinos down below!'

Arx suddenly jumped in the air. 'Iggy, you have given me an idea,' he cried. 'Put the *Sauropod* into a high orbit above Hawn, quickly.'

'Why do you want us to go in circles around the planet?' asked Rosso, pointing to the solawurm growing ever larger on the scanner screen. 'That monster will keep coming after us with its fireballs.'

'No time to explain now,' Arx muttered, frantically working out some sums. 'Just do it, Iggy!'

'No sooner said than done,' Iggy replied. 'We are now three hundred miles above the centre of the planet.'

'Good. Put on the brakes!' Arx commanded.

'Have you gone space crazy?' spluttered Rosso.

But Iggy did as he was told. He trusted Arx with his life. 'Slowing to a stop over Hawn's equator,' he said.

A gulp travelled down Rosso's long throat as another ball of star-fire seared towards them on the scanner screen. 'Incoming!'

'*Move*, Iggy!' Arx cried.

Iggy pulled his special lever once more, and the *Sauropod* sped away as a huge ball of solar energy engulfed the space where they'd been sitting. The star-fire hung there, sizzling.

'Right,' said Arx. 'Travel twenty degrees north and stop again.'

'He *has* gone space crazy!' cried Noss. 'It's like you *want* the solawurm to fire at us.'

'I do! It's your planet's only chance!' Arx cried, as yet another fireball came scorching towards them. 'We just have to hope we can stay ahead of the starfire. Move again, Iggy—another twenty degrees north, ten degrees east . . .'

Iggy wiped a trickle of sweat from his brow and steered them onwards—trying to ignore the scary sight of the bloated solawurm on the scanner still steaming after them . . .

*　　　*　　　*

'Look, there in the distance!' cried Gipsy, pointing through Shuttle Alpha's window. 'It's Grakk. He's flying around Hawn!'

'My poor brother,' said Heelum, propelling himself through space even faster, still dragging the astrosaurs along with his eyelash. 'The planet's last sun is still shining, but see—Grakk has been burping star-fire in all directions!'

Teggs nodded. The space around Hawn was ablaze with balls of dazzling white energy. Then his eyes almost stood out on stalks as he saw the *Sauropod* come whizzing out from under Grakk's smoking, bloated belly. 'Look!'

But Gipsy was already speaking into the communicator. 'Shuttle Alpha to *Sauropod*, can you hear me?'

'Gipsy!' Arx's delighted voice rattled out through the shuttle's speakers. 'Is Captain Teggs all right?'

'Just about.' Teggs pushed up beside Gipsy. 'What's the situation, guys?'

'We've been keeping the solawurm

busy, Captain,' said Iggy. 'But it's not easy— *Whoops!*'

Teggs and Gipsy gasped as they saw Grakk lunge and snap at the *Sauropod* with his smoking jaws. The egg-shaped ship escaped being crushed by a split-second.

'I'm not sure we can keep dodging this thing for ever,' panted Arx.

'But we will try,' Iggy added bravely.

'You're the best,' Teggs told them. He quickly crossed to where Lord Rawhead lay in the corner and shook him awake. 'All right, Lord *Knuckle-head*—how do we set Grakk free from your hypnotic spell?'

'Ha!' The carnivore lord sneered at them. 'I'll never tell. Never, never, NEVER!'

Gipsy walked calmly up to him and rubbed her hooves together. 'I am a luminous green belt in dino-judo,' she informed him. 'If you *don't* tell us, I will jab you somewhere extremely unpleasant—and so hard that your eyes will still be watering several months later.'

'Ah! Well, in that case,' squeaked Rawhead quickly, 'you need to strike Grakk between the eyes. That will shock him out of his trance.'

'Thank you,' said Gipsy sweetly.

Teggs charged back to the communicator. 'Teggs calling Arx— you must hit that solawurm with a dung-torpedo right between the eyes.'

'Sorry, Captain,' said Arx, dodging yet another ball of star-fire launched from Grakk's gigantic jaws. 'We've fired all our weapons. We've got nothing left.'

'And *we* don't have any weapons either,' wailed Gipsy.

A slow, dangerous smile spread over Teggs's face. 'You're forgetting *one* weapon. The shuttle itself . . .' He grabbed the communicator. 'Arx, we are approaching you with a friendly solawurm. Fly straight at us and make sure Grakk follows you. OK?'

'We will do our best, Captain,' said Arx.

Teggs jumped up. Already, the vast, thrashing figure of Grakk was zooming towards them in pursuit of the *Sauropod*. 'Heelum, we need you to throw this shuttle so that it hits Grakk right between the eyes,' he shouted. 'It's the only way to shock him awake before he eats that sun.'

'I haven't thrown anything since I was a wurm-cub playing meteor marbles,' Heelum protested.

'Please, Heelum,' Gipsy begged him. 'You must try.'

'No, he mustn't!' screamed Rawhead. 'If Grakk spots us coming, he will burn us to ashes! And if Heelum misses, we will plunge into the sun!'

'Do it, Heelum,' Teggs shouted. 'NOW!'

The next moment he and Gipsy were flung to the floor as Heelum's eyelash unfurled at high speed—propelling the shuttle through space towards Grakk's pale and furious face . . .

CHAPTER ELEVEN

A NEW DAWN

Whooooosh . . . THUNK!

Shuttle Alpha flew through the fire and smoke surrounding Grakk's face and struck him precisely on target—right between the eyes. Then the shuttle bounced off again and whizzed away into space.

'Whoaaaa!' yelled Teggs and Gipsy.

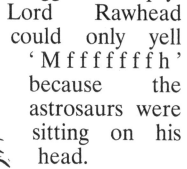

Lord Rawhead could only yell 'M f f f f f f f h' because the astrosaurs were sitting on his head.

'Good thing I was *ruling champion* at meteor marbles, eh?' Heelum told Teggs and Gipsy.

'But we're not out of the woods yet,'

cried Teggs. 'We're out of *control*!'

Gipsy nodded, clinging onto his tail as the shuttle spun wildly about. 'And if we crash into one of those balls of star-fire . . .'

But the next moment, the shuttle stopped spinning and started to slow down. 'What's happening?' wondered Teggs.

He and Gipsy peered out nervously through the window to find . . .

The *Sauropod* was right outside!

'We are using our emergency shuttle magnets to draw you in, Captain,' Iggy explained over the speakers. 'See you soon!'

Teggs grinned at Gipsy as the shuttle floated gently inside the *Sauropod*'s launch bay. They opened the door to find Arx, Iggy and Rosso waiting with broad smiles on their faces, and rushed out to say hello.

But in their happy haste, they had forgotten Lord Rawhead.

'You soppy sap-slurpers!' he growled, shoving them aside and running for the main doors. 'You'll never stop me. I'm going to steal your

ship, and then I'll—'

Suddenly, a skinny, woolly leg stuck out from behind the doorway to trip him up. With a loud '*Argh!*' the megalosaurus went flying again, and fell flat on his face.

'Wow!' said Noss, shuffling into sight. 'The odds against me pulling off that trick must be at least ten million, three hundred thousand and twelve to

one!'

Arx beamed. 'I *told* you there was more to life than calculations!'

Serras appeared behind him. 'Even so, I'm one hundred per cent certain that I will now give you a huge hug!' And she grabbed Noss in a brief but woolly embrace.

'You tripped up Lord Rawhead, Noss—the mastermind behind this evil scheme,' Teggs announced. 'He wanted the entire DSS fleet to come here—now, when they arrive, they can escort him to the nearest space prison!'

'But what about Grakk?' wondered Gipsy, crossing to the launch-bay windows. 'Will Heelum be escorting *him* away from Hawn, or did the shock of our sock on the head not work?'

The others joined her, peering out through the thick glass. They saw that Heelum had wrapped his golden tail around Grakk's swollen middle, as if getting ready to squeeze.

'I am truly sorry for all that my brother has been forced to do,' boomed Heelum's voice in their heads. 'He has eaten too much and is quite

unwell. But now he has been shocked
out of his hypnosis, I think I can make
everyone feel better . . .'

He tightened his tail and squeezed
on the stuffed solawurm's tummy. An
enormous, skull-shaking burp echoed
in their heads, as the dazed Grakk
belched out clouds of solar gasses at
Hawn's one remaining sun.

Serras gasped. 'Our little sun . . . it's getting bigger!'

The astrosaurs and their friends gazed in wonder. As the dazzling stream of brightness flowed out from Grakk's giant jaws, so Hawn Sun Three kept inflating before their eyes. Finally, the unbelievable burp ended, leaving both Grakk and the sun looking a good deal brighter.

'Farewell, dinolings,' said Heelum solemnly. 'We shall go now to the depths of space, never to return . . .'

'Goodbye, Heelum,' said Gipsy fondly.

Teggs saluted him through the window. 'And if you ever come across another pendulum—look the other way!'

The two solawurms disappeared into the endless night of space—taking Lord Rawhead's dreams of conquest with them.

Admiral Rosso breathed a huge sigh of relief.

'Well, all's well that ends well.'

'Are you sure?' asked Teggs. 'Hawn's sun is much bigger and brighter now—but will it be warm enough to make the buttercups grow again?'

'Not on its own, no.' Iggy smiled knowingly. 'But each time Grakk tried to hit the *Sauropod* with his star-fire, Arx made sure we were parked in carefully-chosen spots . . .'

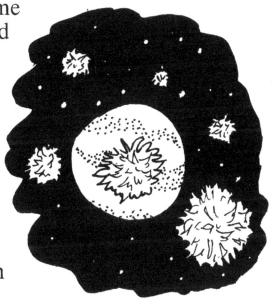

Serras nodded eagerly. 'Thanks to Arx, we now have dozens of burped-up star-fire balls in orbit. They are like baby suns, shining in key positions right the way around the planet.'

Teggs looked out over the bright lights circling Hawn, and grinned. 'So while you may have lost two big suns, you have found lots of little ones!'

Gipsy kissed the blushing triceratops on his head-frill. 'Arx Orano, you are a genius.'

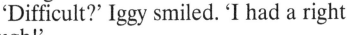

'It was nothing, really,' Arx m u m b l e d. 'Poor Iggy had the difficult job of steering us about.'

'Difficult?' Iggy smiled. 'I had a right laugh!'

Noss wriggled out of his jumper. 'And now, with our main sun bigger and brighter and portable suns warming the sky, Hawn will once again become the buttercup capital of the Vegetarian Sector!'

Serras nodded excitedly and turned to Rosso. 'We must arrange a feast for your entire fleet when they arrive.'

'A short break and a bucket of buttercups would go down *very* nicely!' said Gipsy.

'You've hit the nail on the head

there,' said Arx.

'And soon we'll hit the *jail* with the *Raw*head!' Iggy quipped, patting the battered carnivore beside him.

'What a dreadful joke,' Gipsy groaned. 'But what an amazing adventure.'

Rosso nodded. 'You all deserve to take things easy for a while.'

'Afraid not, sir,' said Teggs with a grin. 'You see, there are two things in life that are absolutely certain. The first thing is that we shall soon be off on *another* amazing adventure . . .'

Gipsy smiled. 'And what's the second thing?'

'That the sun will rise again tomorrow!' said Teggs with a wink.